CRIMINAL CHRISTMAS VOLUME 1

CONNOR WHITELEY

No part of this book may be reproduced in any form or by any electronic or mechanical means. Including information storage, and retrieval systems, without written permission from the author except for the use of brief quotations in a book review.

This book is NOT legal, professional, medical, financial or any type of official advice.

Any questions about the book, rights licensing, or to contact the author, please email connorwhiteley@connorwhiteley.net

Copyright © 2023 CONNOR WHITELEY

All rights reserved.

DEDICATION

Thank you to all my readers without you I couldn't do what I love.

AUTHOR OF THE BETTIE ENGLISH PRIVATE MYSTERIES

CONNOR WHITELEY

CONFESSION IN THE DARKNESS

A WORLD WAR TWO HISTORICAL MYSTERY SHORT STORY

CONFESSION IN THE DARKNESS
27th December 1943

St Paul's Cathedral, London, England

The arid aroma of burning petrol, smoke and smouldering buildings, leaving the taste of burnt food on her tongue, gently filtered through into St Paul's cathedral as French Resistance Leader Marie-Madeline Hall sat on one of the massive cold wooden pews in a row of them that seemed to stretch on endlessly, and the dark, almost black wood of the pews seemed like such a stunning, but stark, contrast against the gently shining gold, silver and bronze of the altar up ahead.

Marie-Madeline had been in England for a good few months now after being flown out of France at the insistence of MI6, the British Spy agency, and her own closest lieutenants, and even now she still found St Paul's to be an impressive reminder of the power of faith in the darkest of hours.

The immense marble altar was a beautiful

reminder of humanity's ability to build and live and worship peacefully without the need to wage a global war against each other, and the massive golden statues and decorative details honouring Christ and many more amazing figures of the bible was another beautiful reminder that Marie-Madeline really needed to savour for the times ahead.

It might have been late in the evening with the only light daring to illuminate St Paul's were a few carefully placed candles that burnt slowly like beacons of hope in the ever-growing darkness that was the war, Marie-Madeline had still been expecting a few more worshippers to honour the cathedral with their presence, especially so close after the Lord Jesus Christ's birthday, the very best of celebrations indeed.

But only Marie-Madeline and another five people were sitting in the pews, and the other five people were so far away sitting on other rows upon rows of pews that she couldn't even really see them clearly. They were mostly women but that was to be expected given the dire state of the war, and Marie-Madeline just wished she had some comfort for them.

She didn't.

Those women were probably here for the exact same reason she was, because she wanted guidance to relax some of her fears about going back to France, her home, the country she loved, and the country she just wanted, needed to be free.

Marie-Madeline was deadly certain that she wanted to go back to France, it was in her blood after all and she never wanted to leave in the first place, but that was before most of her network had fallen, her resources had been destroyed and some of her best friends in the entire world had been captured, and were probably dead now.

Marie-Madeline smiled to herself for a moment because that was exactly why she had to go back to France, because it needed her and Marie-Madeline needed France to be free, and if there was any chance that her friends were still alive then she absolutely had to stop the war and get them back.

No matter the cost.

The sound of footsteps, people muttering prays and a person coughing echoed around the cathedral as Marie-Madeline focused on a very tall man in the black clothes of a priest walk past, and he looked at her and bowed her head.

"Do you need anything dear child?" the Priest asked.

Marie-Madeline wanted to scream and shout *yes* to that question and tell him all of her fears and worries and concerns about returning to France after so long, but if she had learnt anything about being a female leader of a resistance group and operating in a man's world, it was that calmness was a girl's best friend.

"Are you free for confession padre?" Marie-Madeline asked.

The Priest smiled and gestured her to follow him.

Marie-Madeline felt her stomach twist into a

painful knot because this was the first time she was allowing herself to realise just how nervous she was about returning to France.

And she had forbidden herself her processing these emotions for so long she was just scared of what she would say and she what she was going to do about the future.

Because Marie-Madeline just knew what happened tonight could decide the fate of the war.

**

27th December 1943

St Paul's Cathedral, London, England

Even before the war, Marie-Madeline had never really liked confessional booths, and this one might have been in thee St Paul's but it was still just as cramped and small and horrible as all the other booths she had been in over her life travelling the world, but still trying to keep her faith as strong as she possibly could.

Marie-Madeline sat on a very uncomfortable chair in the dark brown confessional booth, and the chair was a little silly in its own right because the "pillow" on it was nothing more than a thin piece of cloth, not exactly comfortable but she wasn't here for comfort, she was here for guidance from God.

The confessional booth wasn't even large enough for Marie-Madeline to stretch her arms out in and the little booth smelt of sweat, dried tears and something musky that Marie-Madeline couldn't identify. She had little doubt the priest had tried to cover up the smell with a faint burning of incense but that did little in reality.

The only advantage of the smell was that Marie-Madeline no longer had to breathe in the horrible aromas of the bombings and attacks on London like she did in the main area of the cathedral.

Marie-Madeline heard someone shuffle around in the booth next to her and moments later, a small panel opened revealing the Priest through a golden metal grate.

And then for the first time Marie-Madeline really focused on the priest, and he was a rather attractive man considering his advanced age, grey hair and his war-hardened face.

Marie-Madeline would have been surprised if the man hadn't fought in the 1914-18 war and now he was just tired of the world fighting itself all over again, Marie-Madeline could really, really understand that.

"Forgive me father for I have sinned, it has been seven days since my last confession," Marie-Madeline said.

"Child of God," the Priest said, "this is a time of war and God testing us, he will forgive you fighting the Devil's influence,"

Marie-Madeline was impressed that the priest seemed to know exactly who she was and what she did. Granted that was hardly surprising given how many of the UK's top politicians, spies and other assets came here, Marie-Madeline would have been surprised if one of them hadn't mentioned her or at least her spy network, considering it was the largest in France.

"God sees all dear Child, what is it that you fear,"

Marie-Madeline didn't want to answer the question, she didn't want to admit to God that she was weaker than others believed her to be, she wasn't sure she could handle the challenges he would throw at her and she really wasn't sure she could undo the Enemy's work in God's divine land.

But she couldn't not answer God.

"I am meant to return to France soon but, I am unsure if I am stronger enough to lead my network after so long. I am not even sure much of it survives," Marie-Madeline said.

The Priest nodded. "God gives us challenges to face but only those that he knows we can face. To doubt the His plan to is to doubt God, and that only leads to damnation dear child,"

Marie-Madeline wanted to disagree, surely doubt was good from time to time. Her doubting her plans and revisiting them and improving her plans had saved her and her network more times than she cared to count, far more times than this priest of all people could possibly understand being locked away in the safety of England for so long.

"You doubt His Plan?" the Priest asked.

Marie-Madeline nodded. "God gives me strength and I don't know how but I know guides my actions but, I don't know how to return to France and win the war for Him,"

Marie-Madeline wasn't exactly sure if she was fighting the war for God per se, but given how she was inside a confessional booth, she knew she just needed to keep sounding zealous enough and maybe the priest would give her a piece of information that was actually useful.

"What are you most scared of dear Child of God?"

Marie-Madeline smiled because ever since the war first started she had only ever had a single fear. Or a range of fears that boiled down to a single deadly point.

"Being captured," Marie-Madeline said.

The Priest nodded fiercely and maybe if she had met him in a "pub" as the English called it, she might have asked what had happened to him in the 1914-18 war, because she had seen the look of horror veterans had all too many times in recent months and that was the exact look the Priest had now.

"God has a plan," the Priest said. "I was captured in the battle of the Somme decades ago, and the Germans tortured, beat and did worse to me. I kept my faith, I kept believing in Him and he rewarded me because he guided the allies to my position and I was freed,"

As much as Marie-Madeline wanted to believe the priest, she just couldn't help but think that maybe God had nothing to do with any of this war and the heroic deeds of it.

Maybe God was just a mythical piece of faith that humans used to keep themselves calm and maybe God wasn't real in the slightest.

"I truly fear His judgement," Marie-Madeline said as she took out two white cyanide tablets that a British spy friend of hers had given her recently just in case.

Marie-Madeline knew that it was logical to want to die instead of falling into enemy hands. Especially as she knew so much about British and French resistance activity, she knew codes and encryptions and the locations of battlegroups.

Marie-Madeline was far too important to fall into enemy hands so surely killing herself was the best way to serve the war effort if it ever came to that.

But Marie-Madeline just couldn't get over the fact that if she killed herself then she was dishonouring God as she was one of his creations and she might go to hell for what seemed like a great idea at the time.

The Priest slowly nodded. "I see your problem dear child of God but know that this is not about dishonouring God it is about something else entirely,"

Marie-Madeline leant closely to the golden metal grate and she really hoped that this was the amazing piece of information that she had been waiting for.

"If you deny the enemy information against the forces of good and people that want to use God's light as a beacon of hope against the darkness. Then this is not dishonouring God, it is simply preventing the enemy and God would forgive you. Jesus sacrificed himself for humanity almost two thousand years ago and now we must all aspire to be as great as he was,"

Marie-Madeline instantly bowed her head slightly as what the priest was saying felt so true, right and real.

And what really surprised her was that Marie-Madeline felt something almost click inside her, like all of her past worries and concerns and fears were disappearing because she knew that God was important, right and he would guide her actions in helping the allies win the war.

No matter how impossible it seemed.

"Thank you padre," Marie-Madeline said.

"May the Lord watch over you," the Priest said as he closed the panel and the golden metal grate disappeared behind a small piece of dark brown wood.

Marie-Madeline sat in the confessional booth for a few more moments and couldn't believe how amazing and light and brilliant she felt, and it was only now that Marie-Madeline was realising how worried she had been earlier.

Marie-Madeline stood up and prepared to leave the confessional booth as a brand new woman, because she had God on her side, and now she was really looking forward to traveling back to France, rebuilding her resistance network and doing exactly what she had been doing so brilliantly for the past four years.

Making sure the British had the best intelligence they could to win the war.

Marie-Madeline opened the wooden door of the confessional booth, lit a candle for all her fallen agents at the altar a few metres away and she simply left St Paul's cathedral descending into the darkness of a busy London street.

Because she had a lot of work to do and she couldn't believe how excited she was to get back to it all, and win her country's freedom once and for all.

AUTHOR OF BETTIE ENGLISH PRIVATE EYE MYSTERIES

CONNOR WHITELEY

PROTECTING CHRISTMAS
A HOLIDAY MYSTERY CRIME SHORT STORY

PROTECTING CHRISTMAS

National Parcel Protection Day (in the US at least) had to be the greatest of Holidays to Jessica, it was a day basically begging for crime to be committed, parcels stolen and their protectors in tears over their failures.

And Jessica was only too happy to oblige.

Jessica wasn't a bad person, she didn't steal for herself, she didn't steal for thrills or any of those so-called excuses, she stole for the good of others.

That reason was a simple excuse according to many of her friends but Jessica loved the holiday season and National Parcel Protection Day most of all, it was her way of giving back.

As Jessica stood in the wonderful little street with small houses packed together with a (rather pathetic) little road separating them, Jessica felt the excitement filling her as she prepared for her first steal of the day.

The air smelt wonderfully of warming Christmas spices, one of the houses were probably baking some mince pies, a little early but each to their own, and Jessica loved the sound of the children singing (badly) at school a few blocks away.

Jessica wasn't sure if she liked the neighbourhood or houses along the street too much. Sure they had Christmas decorations, lights and wreaths hanging all over them. But there was something strange about them, they were all the same, identical and not in a beautiful way.

The bitter cold was another reason Jessica didn't like the neighbourhood, every neighbourhood in England had a certain (extremely varying) degree of charm to it and even the houses that were meant to look alike had their own faults and aspects of character to it.

These houses did not.

If Jessica was to guess, she might have believed some American developer had created this street or something but she didn't know. And she most certainly didn't want to find out. This street felt weird.

The wonderfully spice scented air got stronger and Jessica licked her lips as she imagined their amazing fruity, spicy taste in her mouth. Maybe she would have to steal some for herself.

Jessica hated that idea. That was flat out wrong, stealing for oneself was never good and Jessica had learnt that first hand as a child.

As a homeless child living, eating and stealing on the streets, she had to get food somehow but she stole from the wrong baker one day, and ended by getting beaten within an inch of her life because of it.

When she recovered, got a job a few years later and learnt that her true family had died in a car crash and left her some money, Jessica vowed to help those on the streets like no one had ever done for her.

The sound of the children singing started to die down as the howl of the bitter wind grew. That was probably the worse thing about the streets, their cold unloving nature. Maybe she would buy some thick coats for the homeless with the money she got from today's theft.

The sound of a large white van driving slowly down the street made Jessica stare at it. Jessica wasn't a fan of white vans, they reminded her too much of scary child kidnapping films and there was something about the speed of the van.

The van shouldn't have been driving that slowly, the entire street was perfectly clean of cars, so the van was hardly going to bump into anything.

Jessica stepped back a little and focused on the drivers. There was one man wearing a black tracksuit and a black cap covering most of his face, and a tall woman was wearing a long black coat.

But what Jessica didn't like was how they were looking each house up and down and around.

That look was all too familiar to Jessica, she had given the entire road those looks twice today already. She had calculated from a bit of research that the post people always come at 12 o'clock on this road like clockwork.

It was almost time and all the houses in the road were empty.

Jessica wasn't sure what the people in the van were doing but she didn't like it. She wanted to go over there, pound on the window and get them to go. This was her road to steal from and at least she was going to give her stolen items to a good cause.

These people weren't, Jessica had run into these sorts of people before. White van drivers that were thieves were never good people to get involved with.

If she could just get one parcel without those people seeing her, then she could get something for the homeless people.

The sound of the van doors slamming shut made Jessica's eyes widen as she saw the man and woman leant against the van and stare at her.

Jessica didn't know what to do. She could run, but she didn't want to be chased.

"You wanna parcel?" the man asked.

Jessica was surprised by his deep, disease ridden voice. He definitely wasn't the healthiest man she had ever met, but there was something creepy about him. The way he stared at her and bit his lip.

"Ah come on Luv," the man said, gesturing her to come close.

Jessica wasn't sure why they were here. If the man and woman had been here for parcels then they should have waited in the van, seen the post people leave the parcels and then steal them.

But they wanted Jessica to come closer to them.

She didn't like this one bit.

"I've got some presents in my van ya can have," the man said.

Jessica's mouth dropped. This man and woman were foul people, they wanted to kidnap her. Jessica was shocked. How dare they come to this street, on her favourite National Day and try to pull a stunt like this.

The sound of children cheering echoed around the neighbour from the school.

"Leave!" Jessica shouted.

She wasn't going to let them kidnap a child if that was their plan, if the local school was finishing earlier today then Jessica was never going to let one of the children anywhere near these people.

Jessica had almost been stolen herself on the streets before, she was never ever going to let another child experience that!

"We ain't doing anything wrong. We just waiting outside out van," the woman said.

Jessica sneered at them both. "What's your plan then? Steal a few children. Get their parents to pay you. Then have a merry Christmas,"

The man and woman smiled at each other.

"What is it to ya?" the man asked.

"I will not let you steal children on my day!"

The man laughed. "Ya Day? What are ya the Queen?"

Queen Jessica, it did have a nice ring to it. But as much as Jessica loved that idea, she had to try to do something today of all days. The holiday was meant to be about Protection after all.

"Go now or I *will* call the police," Jessica said.

The man mockingly cried. "Ya really think ta police will show up for two peeps leaning against a van,"

Jessica wanted to protest but that was a harsh truth about the world they lived in. Years of cut backs, politics and everything had left all public services decimated to varying degrees, the police was no less affected than any other public service.

After spending about ten years as a police call handler Jessica remembered that all too well.

"Tell ya what luv. Leave. We let you live," the man said.

Jessica shook her head. "I am not leaving you two alone,"

"Come on, you must have some fam. Ready want 'em to receive your ransom?" the woman said.

Jessica was glad she didn't have any still alive. She hated her true family for abandoning her and when they died it was almost joyous to her. But how dare these idiots threaten her, they were going to be in for a hell of a surprise. She had lived on the streets long enough to learn how to defend herself.

The amazing smell of warm mince pies made Jessica realise there had to be someone at home in one of the houses, maybe if she was loud enough they would check on the situation.

But what would it look like?

She wasn't sure. All it probably looked like were two strange people leaning against a van and a crazy woman who clearly wasn't from the neighbourhood shouting at them.

"My family wouldn't pay for pay anyway," Jessica said.

The man grabbed his genitals. "I would luv,"

That was the final straw, Jessica had to do something. This man was disgusting and it was even more disgusting that this lady friend (girlfriend, wife, mistress?) wasn't saying anything.

Then Jessica remembered how cruel both men and women can be to homeless children on the street.

Jessica looked at her watch. It was a few minutes to twelve. The post people would be here soon, maybe that could save her and the children.

"You need to go now!" Jessica shouted, tapping her watch.

The man grinned. "Ya think ta postman is gonna stop us. We'll just gut him, like we will ya!"

The man whipped out a knife.

The woman did the same.

Jessica froze.

They both ran at her.

Her street training kicked in.

The man swung.

Jessica ducked.

Slamming her fists into his jaw.

He moaned.

Jessica kicked the woman in the chest.

She screamed.

The man swung again.

Quickly.

There were too many strikes coming.

Jessica ducked.

She rolled.

She jumped up.

Smashing her fists into the man's spine.

Something cracked.

The woman swung.

Jessica punched her.

The knife almost cutting her.

The woman jumped forward.

Knocking Jessica to the ground.

The knife sliced her.

The woman attacked again.

Thrusting the knife into Jessica's chest.

She screamed.

Jessica grabbed the woman's hands.

Forcing the knife to remain in her.

The woman looked scared.

Jessica headbutted her.

She let go of the knife.

Jessica whacked the woman.

She fell to the ground.

Jessica stomped on her head.

The man got up.

Jessica kicked him in the head.

Jessica frowned at the man and woman on the ground with blood on their face and a wave of discomfort washed over Jessica as she feared they were dead. She never wanted to kill them.

Jessica checked their pulses.

To her relief both the man and the woman were unconscious and not dead. A very small part of her wanted them dead, at least that way they wouldn't be able to hurt any more children ever again.

But the truth for Jessica was she wasn't a killer. Even during her darkest days on the streets, she never hurt anyone who didn't deserve it.

She bit her lip as a wave of pain from the stab wound washed over her. Jessica pressed the wound gently and she was relieved that it wasn't bleeding, it wasn't a bad cut and at least she would still be around to help the homeless.

The sound of police sirens in the distance was almost angelic to Jessica as that had to be a sign that the children would be safe and these two would be sent to prison. At least she had somehow honoured her favourite National Day, whilst she didn't have any presents for the homeless people today, at least she had protected the innocent from these idiots.

And that was a good day in her books.

The sound of the police sirens were getting closer so Jessica went up to the back of the white van, kicked the lock and opened it for the police.

Jessica was shocked at all the rope, candies and comic books that the two creeps had both for the children. She was more than glad she had stopped them now and at least the police could clearly see that the man and woman were the bad guys, and not her.

As Jessica walked off into the distance leaving the police to find the man, woman and the incriminating white van, Jessica was filled with delight that her National Parcel Day had gone so perfectly.

She was going to remember this for a long, long time.

AUTHOR OF BETTIE ENGLISH PRIVATE EYE SERIES

CONNOR WHITELEY

CHRISTMAS THIEF

A JANE SMITH AMATEUR SLEUTH MYSTERY SHORT STORY

CHRISTMAS THIEF

Amateur Sleuth Jane Smith just loved Christmas more than any other time of the year (maybe except for her children's birthdays), there was so much amazing magic about Christmas, and of course Jane loved the food, presents and family too.

Ever since she had been a kid, Jane had always been obsessed with Christmas, it was fun, exciting and she loved eating her way through the season, and then when she had kids, her love for the season only grew in intensity.

Every year Jane would make sure her kids got the best Christmas they possibly could, and even with the kids leaving home and returning to Jane's small village in the south of England with their families for Christmas, she still tried her hardest to make it rememberable.

As Jane placed the freshly made Christmas cake on the wooden worktop of her kitchen, Jane took deep wonderful breaths of the cake's amazing aroma that made the house smell of rich fruits, sugar and more than enough alcohol to knock out a horse.

Jane just admired the cakes great brown colour, rich fruit and everything about the cake was just wonderful. To Jane this was the start of the holiday season, making the cake in early December was just perfect and it showed her that she needed to start getting her bum in gear about the rest of it.

Jane listened to the wonderful quiet singing in the background of Christmas songs that she had playing on her record player, she had tried to download something called *mp3s* before, but they never sounded as good as real records.

As Jane's kitchen started to fill up with steam, she went over to one of the windows that lined a wall of the kitchen and she popped it open. When the cold breeze rushed past her, Jane realised how hot it was in the kitchen, and that made her smile as that was always a part of Christmas.

Christmas had to be cold for Jane.

When her two kids were really young, her and her husband had taken them to America for Christmas, but everyone had hated it because Christmas was so over the top in America, and it was so hot. Christmas wasn't about money or heat to Jane, it was about love, food and family, some points that trip completely failed on.

A knock at the front door made Jane hiss as she made sure her wonderful Christmas cake was perfectly level on the worktop, she wasn't going to have hours of work (and cooking fun) drop onto the floor if she could help it.

Jane went through her house, into the little hallway and opened her front door to see her best friend standing there in the freezing cold, shaking.

"Come in Marg,"

"Thanks Pet," Marg said as she walked in and Jane led her out into the kitchen.

Jane popped on the kettle and pointed to a small round table that she had tucked away into the corner of the kitchen and Marg pulled out one of the chairs underneath and sat down.

But the kitchen was a lot colder than she remembered, she made a mental note to shut the window in a moment.

Jane had to admit she hadn't been expecting her best friend today, she had definitely hadn't expected her to walk from the other side of the village in the freezing cold to see her. Jane didn't know whether to be happy or concerned.

"Nice cake Pet,"

"Thanks," Jane said, as she finished making the tea and bought it over to Marg, "Why you here? Wasn't expecting you today,"

"Yea Pet. I just wanna…" Marg said.

Jane stared at her best friend out of concern more than anything because Marg never just trailed off, but then Jane realised Marg wasn't staring at her, she was staring past her at the cake.

Jane turned around and gasped when she saw

half the Christmas Cake had been… cut away and was gone. Someone had stolen her legendary Christmas cake.

"Why did ya cut the cake Pet?"

"I… I didn't. It was piping hot before you knocked on the door. It was right there,"

"Are ya sure Pet? I thought only yesterday I had made myself a sandwich and ate it, turned out I made myself some soup and binned it instead,"

Jane wanted to say how old, silly and forgetful Marg had become in her old age, but as much as she wanted to, Jane loved her best friend far, far too much to be that mean to her.

"That didn't happen,"

"Good Pet, because you would look like a right idiot for doing that,"

Jane just smiled as she stood up and went over to the cake. It looked perfectly cooked in the middle with perfect fruit distribution and the most perfect crumb Jane had ever seen. This was going to be an amazing cake on Christmas day.

It was just annoying that someone had dared to steal some from her!

"Shut that window pet please,"

Jane nodded and looked at the window and she just folded her arms. This was getting ridiculous, the window earlier than only been opened a little bit but now it was wide open, letting a massive draft come in.

Jane went into one of her cupboards and took out some plain flour, sprinkling it around the window to check for fingerprints.

There were none.

But there was the top of a black leather glove caught in-between the window and the hinges. Jane carefully took it out and smelt it. The awful scents of cheap female perfume filled her nose as she passed it to Marg to examine.

"This ain't good Pet," Marg said, "someone stole my cake,"

Jane laughed and she agreed. Marg was always her first taste tester and… oh that was why Marg had come round today, and Jane just playfully hit Marg on the head.

"Figured it out then Pet?"

"You're terrible,"

"I'm hungry that's what pet,"

As Jane went into the cupboard and got Marg a pack of biscuits, she couldn't help but feel her stomach tighten at the idea that someone had stolen some cake from her.

And for what?

Jane had to figure it out, because she couldn't fail her family for Christmas, she had to get the Christmas cake back from the thief or she feared more than anything else, that Christmas would be ruined for her family.

And Jane hated that idea.

***

After finishing her wonderful cup of strong tea that was so strong it almost burnt her mouth, Jane sat at the round table in her kitchen and wondered about the piece of ripped glove.

It didn't seem right in the slightest, it was clear that it had come from the thief, but what Jane couldn't understand was why steal the cake in the first place? And why only take half of it?

Jane watched Marg finish off her packet of biscuits and she almost wished she hadn't had given them to Marg, she loved those chocolate biscuits and now she was out.

"You know Pet," Marg said, "the thief was clever not to take it all,"

Jane cocked her head. "How?"

"Cos I knew you were making the cake today. If I walked in Pet, and the cake wasn't here, I would have known,"

Jane was actually surprised at her friend's logic and maybe that was the key to it. Jane couldn't remember if she had told anyone else about her famous Christmas cake, or where she and Marg were when Jane told Marg about the cake baking today?

Maybe other people could have heard.

"Where were we when I told you?" Jane asked.

"I donna Pet. Maybe the corner shop two days ago," Marg said nodding.

Jane completely agreed as that was when she had picked up an extra packet of icing because she doubted the pre-roll stuff she bought would be big enough for when she iced it in a few weeks.

"The corner shop wasn't very busy, was it?"

Marg finished off her tea. "No Pet. It was you, me and... Bourbon Creams too and the shop keeper,"

Jane clicked her fingers at Marg, she had actually spoken to the woman everyone in the village called Bourbon Creams because whenever anyone saw her, the woman always carried round and offered everyone a Bourbon Cream from her tub.

"Do you think she stole my cake?" Jane asked.

"Ha!" Marg shouted by accident. "Come on Pet, she only eats Bourbon Creams, she doesn't eat cake. And she's gluten free or something,"

Jane's eyes widened as she realised why Bourbon Creams' biscuits always tasted so amazing.

"Do you think she told anyone?"

"Yes," Marg said, "Pet, remember when you caused the massive cake fight of 99 at the cooking club before Christmas?"

Jane slowly nodded, she had completely forgotten about all the cakes that had been thrown, kicked and smashed that fateful night on New Years eve 1999.

"Well Pet, some of the ladies never forgave you for winning the cake of the Century award. Two of those women are still alive and Bourbon Creams eats with them weekly,"

"Weekly?" Jane asked, "As in the past few days,"

"Oh yes Pet," Marg said as she went over to the kettle, "I saw them yesterday in the little Turkish place off the high street. They were talking about

Christmas cakes, come to think of it,"

Jane couldn't believe these awful women would want to steal from her. But Jane could understand it all, because on New Years Eve 1999, the two women (sisters actually) have both baked their own famous sponge cakes, and then Jane turned up with her leftover Christmas Cake and won.

Jane smiled as she remembered how furious they had gotten about it all, she was fairly sure her husband even got a broken nose out of it, those two sisters were vicious.

"Smell this again," Jane said, passing Marg the glove as she sat back down with a freshly made cup of tea.

Marg smelt it. "Yea pet, that what they smell like,"

Jane stood up and smiled. This was exactly the sort of thing she needed and wanted, she was going to go to those sisters and get her cake back, Jane was never going to allow these people to spoil Christmas for her family.

Jane was going to get the cake back (and answers) no matter what.

Even if she had to be unladylike about it!

***

With Marg shuffling behind her, Jane marched up to the black front door of where the Sisters lived and pounded on it hard.

Jane was furious.

The sisters lived in such an ugly part of the

village with its rundown houses and even the sisters' stone house was cracking and falling apart. Jane was going to make them pay for stealing from her! That was a promise, not a threat!

After a few moments, the door opened and two large brutish looking women stepped outside. Jane hated their saggy-muscular builds and their poorly aged face and long grey hair.

Jane had thought they looked great last century, but they clearly hadn't been looking after themselves.

The slightly taller sister frowned at Jane. "What you want!"

Jane had to force herself not to run away, the idea of these two women beating her up kept playing through her mind, but she had to stay firm and get back her cake.

"Give me my cake back. I know you stole it. I can prove it,"

"Bugger off," the sisters said.

They went to shut the door and Jane slammed her foot in-between the door and the frame.

Pain flooded up her leg but she forced her face not to show it.

"Bugger off!" the sisters shouted as they cracked their knuckles.

"Come on Pets don't be stupid," Marg said shuffling up behind Jane.

The sisters smiled. "Two on two. That's a bit fairer,"

Jane forced Marg back as the two sisters walked

out of their house, cracking their knuckles. Jane wasn't going to let them hurt Marg.

"Stop Pets!" Marg shouted.

The two sisters' eyes widened. Jane turned around to see Marg taking out a little black device with a red flashing light on it.

"What that?" the sisters asked.

"If I press this, the police come. It's an OAP distress signal, it's a powerful thing, I always take it with me Pets," Marg said.

The sisters looked at each other. "We'll knock 'em out before that happens,"

Marg gestured she was going to press it. "I'll do it Pets. Don't be such mugs,"

Jane really didn't know what to do, she knew Marg was lying, but she had to save herself, Marg and save Christmas for her family. She just didn't know how.

The Sisters walked forward.

"I pressed it!" Marg shouted as the red flashing light got faster and faster.

The Sisters looked around. They were sweating. One of them rushed into the house.

"Give us the recipe and we'll square," the remaining sister said.

Jane shook her head. "No, my grandmother gave me the recipe and you stole from me. If you had asked, I would have given it to you, but not now. Not ever,"

The remaining sister spat at Jane's feet. "Don't

need it anyway. We ate it. It good. Now bugger off,"

As the other sister rushed back out of the house, holding a tiny piece of something in tin foil, Jane felt her stomach tighten as she knew she had failed. That half of her Christmas cake was gone.

The sisters vomited.

Jane shot back.

She covered Marg's eyes.

The sisters kept vomiting.

Vomit painted the pathway.

As the sounds of sirens filled the air, Jane's eyes widened as she watched the two sisters drop to their knees in front of their own house as they gasped for air in-between the violent waves of vomiting.

Jane smiled as two police officers walked past and just looked at Jane and Marg.

"Be a dear officer and call an ambulance," Jane said.

***

As Jane took out a brand new cake from the oven and placed it on a wire cooling rack on her kitchen worktop, she couldn't believe how amazing the air smelt, hints of warming spices, rich fruit and almost no alcohol filled the air as Jane went back over to the little table in the kitchen.

Marg was sitting there nursing a large mug of coffee as if it was whiskey, but after hearing back from the police officers and watching them siege all Jane's alcohol, she knew both of them would stay far, far, far away from alcohol this Christmas season.

It turned out Jane had misread the recipe and added in extreme levels of alcohol, and all her alcohol had gone off and turned bad, so it was no surprise to the paramedics that after eating half the Christmas cake, the two sisters had vomited.

And in reality Jane was extremely glad the theft had taken place, if the sisters hadn't stolen the cake then maybe Marg, herself and even Jane's amazing family would have been sick.

Jane shook those thoughts away, she couldn't handle the idea of anything bad happening to any of them, she loved Marg as much as her own children. She was part of the family, Jane was never ever going to let anything happen to her.

But at least sisters had learnt consequences for their actions, they were clearly horrible people and Jane (as bad as it sounded) was glad they had been violently sick, no one got to mess with her Christmas, Marg or her family and got to get away with it without punishment.

Then Jane noticed Marg was smiling at her and flicking her eyes between Jane and the Christmas Cake, if it had been anyone else, Jane would have said no. But this was Marg, her amazing friend that she would do anything for and protect until the end.

As Jane went over to the cake and cut them both a small slice, she realised this was going to be a great start to an amazing holiday season.

CHRISTMAS, CRIME, LETTER

Elizabeth State was dead, but now she lives again.

Of course she wasn't really, that would just be silly. But in a strange way she was alive once more through me, as it was her identity that my guy gave me for tonight's rather... lavish party and my theft.

I stood in the massive white room with walls reaching high into the sky and stretching as far back as I could see, and in the middle of the room there was a rather... interesting (tasteless) column with two sets of stone stairs spiralling around that, leading to two exhibition rooms.

My targets.

Now I called this the opening area of the British Museum (there probably was an official name but I didn't care).

If I was alone in here then I would definitely have taken advantage, stealing from the food court that was on the far, far side of the room and maybe even stealing from the gift shop that was rumoured to be around here.

But sadly I wasn't.

I was surrounded by the snobs of the almighty rich and powerful of the Museum's largest donators, and when I mean largest I do mean it. I don't know how some of these donators would fit on their private jets or even get into buildings. They were walking, talking, smelly tanks.

Thankfully they were some thinner donators too!

Yet I must admit watching most of these stunning fit rich men in their tight black suits, smooth faces and expensive haircuts, it was almost enough to make a woman fluster and turn red.

But I am nothing short of professional. I am here to do a theft after all.

I grabbed a glass of golden champagne and circulated through the crowd, since the most amateur mistake you can make is to survey the entire room from one spot. That's what all the security guards watch for.

The sounds of the rich men and women talking, laughing and snorting filled my ears as I circulated the room. Looking out for security guards, undercovers and any more surprises.

Now my theft was marvellous because in the spirit of National Letter Writing Day (in the US at least), the Museum had decided to host some silly party for their largest (and thinnest) donators to unveil the first ever letter written to Father Christmas, or whatever the German for Father Christmas is, as it was apparently written there.

Normally I never ever bother with such small prizes. I'm more into sparkling, dazzling and millionaire treasures, but my client mentioned that the letter was worth a few million to him, so who was I to argue with such a refined (and foul) character?

And because this theft is technically for a wonderful holiday, I bought my small golden purse packed with a few wonderful surprises for anyone who tries to stop me.

Anyway I need a few quid these days for my sick mother, so I'm not exactly in a position to be too fussy with work. Then the rest of the money I'll probably keep some, donate some more to charity. I might even donate some to the museum.

Ha! Fat chance!

The sound of people shuffling caught my attention as I followed the crowds of (hot) young men and some other women towards the front of the room. Then I simply glided to the back of the crowd so I could watch everyone as we all stared at this posh elderly man who stood (way too) proudly on the stone steps.

I coughed a few times as I smelt all the horrible scents of aftershaves, perfumes and whatever unholy concoction these rich snobs covered their bodies in. I mean this is just ridiculous. A few sprays is fine fair enough, but an entire bottle! I don't want to choke to death on their smell!

As the elderly man starting to thank the donators, making a few awful jokes that only the snobbish manners of the rich would understand and introducing the letter. I started to notice a rather stunning man standing next to me.

He looked amazing in his custom-made tight black suit, his smooth handsome face and his stunning movie star smile. He seemed to be listening intently to the elderly man, but I didn't recognise him.

You see, I always make it a job before a job to memorise everyone's faces so I know exactly who will be there.

This hot guy wasn't meant to be here.

A drop of sweat rolled down my back. Now I had to play it cool, I couldn't act rash or question this guy because he would know what I was. And if he wasn't another thief then that would be a major cock-up on my part.

Believe me I may have done that before. Not a good idea.

The man leant closer to me. "You look beautiful tonight,"

If this man was simply a rich donator who wanted to unzip my dress then that would be okay, but there was something about this guy.

"Don't look so bad yourself," I said.

"What's your plan to get the letter? I was thinking about a simple fire alarm trick," the man said.

This guy might have been a thief, or he was lying which was my guess, but he couldn't have been a very good one given the letter was stored in a protected environment and extra security protocols were activated by the fire alarm.

"I don't know what you're talking about," I said, focusing on the speaker who looked like he was wrapping up.

"Who have you come as this time, Madame Francis?"

I felt my smile disappear as he said the name of one of my old aliases, he must have known of me for ages considering that one was from a job in France maybe… five years ago. At least I still had my escape routes if needed.

The stunning man stepped in front of me and

looked at my name badge, not that it would give him anything too useful.

"Elizabeth State, good name. She died ten years ago in the Caribbean you know,"

Now I ready wanted to leave, this guy knew way, way, way too much for being a simple rich man at a party. The man felt safe and good enough but there was something about him. He was hot as hell and yes, I would love him to unzip my dress tonight, but there was something off.

I went close to his ears, savouring the amazing smell of his aftershave.

"I presume you're a cop,"

The man almost laughed. "No, no Elizabeth. I not a cop. I see you haven't got my letter yet,"

I took a few steps back. This man couldn't have been my client, on the phone my client sounded older, richer and nowhere near as sexy.

The man kept smiling and changed his voice.

"In the package there will be an invitation and a dress. Go to the party, get the target and drop it off on the third seat of the Ten O'clock Tube at the nearest station,"

This wasn't right. They were the exact words of my client, but now this made no sense to me. I was well renowned as a master thief and yet my client felt the need to tail me to this event. They must have known I could get the letter-

The elderly man finished and started leading everyone up into the exhibition hall where the letter was.

I and this stunning but annoying as hell man followed.

"I wasn't expecting you here. But my fee is

doubled," I said.

The man frowned.

"I did tell you on my website. No tails. You must have read the terms and conditions?"

The man muttered something.

In truth I didn't have any terms, conditions or contracts on the site, but my clients always believed it. The amazing stupidity of the rich!

The crowd led me into a slightly smaller white room with the walls covered in breath-taking depictions of Christmas traditions through the centuries. From the pagans that started Christmas as we know it all the way to the wonderful (and far better) secular Christmases that we all know and love today, in all but name.

As the crowd of rich men and women slowly went around the room reading the stuff on the walls, my eyes were immediately drawn to the large glass cabinet in the middle of the room.

And inside it was a large, very long letter to Father Christmas in perfect condition and all written in German.

It was hard to believe that such a thing was worth so much money, but this hot as hell man clearly wanted it.

Then the idiot hot man decided to start walking straight over to the letter. Idiot!

I went over to him, wrapped my arm round his and guided him away.

"Oh honey, wait. We can look at the letter later, I want to read about Pagan festivals first," I said, shaking my head and smiling at my pretend lover.

The man smiled and went close to my ear. "What are you doing?"

"Oh honey, you've never done this before have you,"

"Never,"

If this was any other guy, I would easily make up some lame excuse to take him outside, then I would hit him, because this is my operation, my theft, my life and this idiot was going to muck it up.

Sadly this man was way too hot to hit and I wished I run my hands under that tight amazing suit and through his wonderfully thick hair, and his lips looked so soft, so warm, so-

The man started to guide me back over to the letter. This was getting out of hand.

"Listen," I said firmly. "No self-respecting thief goes for the prize straight away. That is how you get caught,"

The man stopped, kissed my head and pretended to talk about the pagan festivals.

"And I can see exactly what I need from here," I said.

"Like what?"

"There are five security guards. One in each corner and an undercover by the letter. The ones in the corners aren't a problem. The crowd is too thick and would delay them,"

"Who's the problem?" the man said, a little too enthusiastically for my taste.

"The one in the middle. He would get to us too quick,"

The man rubbed my arm as a few people looked at us. My fingers against my arm felt amazing, pure electricity flowed through me, I was enjoying him way too much.

"What about the glass cabinet itself? Looks

harmless," he asked.

Again if this was anyone else, I would have told them to break the cabinet, whilst I slipped into the crowd and let them get arrested. But sadly this stunning man was actually growing on me.

"Don't be stupid. The cabinet is electrified, it has a motion sensor and a heat sensor built into the case,"

The man frowned. "I thought you could break it,"

Now that was offensive!

"What do you take me for?" I asked.

"A hack,"

How I didn't slap him then I don't know.

A tall waitress was coming towards us with glasses of wonderfully golden champagne.

"Grab a glass," I said firmly.

We both grabbed one.

I couldn't help my smile but the next part was going to be great fun. Normally I did the whole acting chaos stuff with actual strangers but it might be even more fun acting with a person who I actually found attractive.

This was going to be fun.

"Are you a good actor?" I asked.

The man looked more concerned. "I suppose so. I did a few school plays. Lead role,"

Oh yes, this man was definitely rich. Only the rich snobs of the world ever compare school plays with proper acting and the level of acting needed for cons.

"Just play along. Go over and stand by the letter," I said.

We went over. Now the fun could begin!

I went over to him. "What are you doing! You

are so obsessed with this stupid letter!"

"Go away woman. Leave me alone for once in your miserable life. In fact. Get a life!"

"How dare you! I didn't even want to come to this shit hole museum tonight!" I shouted.

"Just go. Go back to our sorry ass kids. They're yours anyway. I don't want you, I don't want them. Now leave!"

The crowd muttered stuff.

"Maybe I will. Maybe I'll get a divorce!"

I went closer to the glass cabinet.

"Do whatever and take those bitching kids with you!"

The crowd didn't like that.

The security guards came over.

The man threw the champagne glass at me.

I ducked.

It splashed over the glass cabinet.

The security guards grabbed him. Taking him outside.

He smiled.

I pretended to cry and the elderly man in his tight suit from his speech on the steps came over and rubbed my back.

"Miss, I am so sorry you had to go through that,"

I hugged him. "And I'm so sorry for those horrible words I said. Your museum is lovely,"

I wiped a few tears away.

"Thank you. Now please stay and enjoy yourself. All five security guards will be downstairs making sure he stays away,"

As the elderly man left, I actually felt a little sad that that hot as hell stunning man wasn't going to be allowed back in. I was actually missing him!

But I did have a job to do, so onto stage two.

I went over to the glass cabinet and double checked if it was possible to see if any of the champagne had got inside.

It wasn't possible to tell. Good!

A rich young couple stood next to me so I whispered to them.

"I think the letter's damaged. I think there's champagne in there,"

The young woman looked horrified. She was clearly a history and art buff so she was perfect for this part. She rushed off to find the elderly man.

When she returned she was in a terrible (to her, wonderful to me) state and was begging the elderly man to open the glass cabinet to check on the *historical integrity* of the letter (Oh yes, she was one of those people).

The elderly man took out a key card from his suit pocket and swiped it over the glass cabinet. The cabinet hummed, vibrated and hissed as the pressurised air escaped. Making the air smell horribly of mustard.

Then the elderly man took off the glass and exposed the letter for all to see.

This was my chance.

I opened my gold purse, cracked a vial and waited.

The elderly man inspected the letter without picking it up.

The young woman and man were talking to the elderly man. He was distracted, my exit was clear.

I grabbed a small breath refresher from my purse filled with knock gas and I sprayed the three of them.

I grabbed the letter.

And run out.

I run down the stairs, past the security guards and out into the night.

***

A few hours later I stood on the cold lonely platform of the Tube Station with no one else there and only the cold concrete and white tiled walls to keep me company. Like every Tube Station after hours, the station smelt like urine, sick and spoiled food, but there was something refreshing about it tonight.

The foul smell kept me alert as I waited for the train and then I could easily escape into the chaos of London, change my identity and begin anew.

If it sounded like a lonely life, that was because it was in a way. It was partly why I did these jobs, thefts and other crazy things, because it meant I got to meet people and experience things that I never would be able to otherwise.

But tonight was surprisingly nice actually. I had never wanted to spend time with anyone before but that hot sexy man with his tight black suit, smooth handsome face and his amazing haircut. I really, really wanted him.

I wanted him to unzip my dress, run my fingers through his hair and down his suit to where my parcel could be delivered.

But I guess that was never going to happen, so again I would be alone doing random jobs over Christmas trying to raise more money for my sick mother, myself and the various charities that I'll donate to.

The sound of the Tube train in the distance made me step towards the edge of the platform as I waited for it to arrive when an arm wrapped round my waist.

I would recognise that amazing aftershave and those strong arms anywhere. That hot, sexy man had returned to me.

"You did well. My Letter?" the man asked.

I smiled and passed him the letter.

He ripped it up.

"What!" I shouted, as the pieces of the letter blew across the rails.

"Relax beautiful. The Letter's fake. I wrote it, aged it and donated it to the Museum. I only wanted to check if it was a good enough forgery,"

All I could do was stare at that amazing movie star smile as he probably felt really pleased with himself, and I couldn't blame him. Fooling the British Museum was no easy feat but he had to be here for something.

"You think I'm beautiful?" I asked.

As the train rolled into the station, the driver probably shocked that there were people here at all, that amazing hot sexy man kissed me on the lips. Hard. I savoured his soft lips and wondered what else was he hiding.

But at least I had my answer. He did find me beautiful, and I him.

I was half expecting him to say something but he gave me a smile. Not a malice, deceptive or evil smile that I would have expected for a forger and fellow criminal. But a smile that a schoolboy gives his prom date when he truly loves her.

He might have been a strange, hot, sexy criminal man who I barely knew, but as the train doors opened and we both went on, I looked forward to seeing where the train was going to lead us and hopefully our journey wouldn't end for a long, long time.

PRIVATE EYE, CONVENTION AND CHRISTMAS

"What's EyeFoodCon aunty?"

When Bettie heard her nephew Sean ask her that simple question, she wasn't really sure how to answer it. As a private eye she had just known what it was for as long as she could remember.

Bettie looked at her tall slim nephew and tried to think about how to answer such a strange question, that she knew what it was, she just didn't know how to explain it to someone who wasn't a private eye.

The sounds of people talking, chatting and laughing on the awfully cold December night made Bettie shiver. She hated the cold so she pulled her long black overcoat tighter and ignored her nephew.

As much as Bettie loved him, she wanted, needed to buy herself a few extra seconds so she could think of an answer to his question.

Bettie watched the little families walk around with the occasional parent moaning at their overexcited kids and other people were weighed down with their Christmas shopping in Bluewater shopping centre in southeast England.

She was glad her and Sean hadn't bought that much stuff tonight but she did need to press on with their shopping. That was probably the only downside to the Christmas season, even more so as a private eye, there were so many cases at Christmas time that it made Christmas shopping in advance impossible.

Bettie bit her lip as she wondered how many more presents she needed to buy. There was her sister, her boyfriend and more.

As she pushed those panicked thoughts away, Bettie watched the busy crowd around them go in and out of shops like their lives depended on it, it seemed them too needed to get lots of presents before the big day.

The smell of rich Christmas spices filled the air as Bettie and Sean kept walking on, gliding through the crowd and walking like they were on a mission. Because in a way they were, Bettie had to get all the presents tonight considering the all the private eye parties started soon.

With the smell of the Christmas spices getting stronger with hints of sweat that made her mouth taste of Christmas cake, Bettie kept gliding through the crowd as her eyes narrowed for the next shop she needed.

"What's EyeFoodCon aunty?" Sean asked again walking next to her.

Bettie smiled. "It's hard to explain Sean. It's a little private holiday for private eyes,"

"Is it like a Christmas party?"

Bettie stepped out of the way of a big family of shoppers and saw a massive wonderful sign in the distance of a perfume shop she needed to go to for her sister. She had no idea why her sister wanted some expensive perfume that she was never going to wear, but Bettie just wanted to keep the peace, love her sister and get on with the rest of the shopping.

The only problem was the sea of busy (grumpy) shoppers in her way.

"Aunty?" Sean asked.

Bettie took Sean's hand like she did when he was a toddler and guided him through the sea of people.

"In a way yes," Bettie said. "It was started a few years back by the Jewish and Muslim private eyes,"

Bettie gently knocked a shopper out of the way so her and Sean could continue through the crowd.

"They heard all their private eye friends were busy and missing over Christmas as they were celebrating with the family. So the Professional Private Investigator Society created EyeFoodCon as a secular celebration for everyone,"

"Ah," Sean said.

After making it through the massive sea of grumpy, busy shoppers, Bettie loved the amazing smell of the sweet flowery perfume in the massive shop she entered.

Bettie cocked her head for a moment as she

didn't remember the shop being this big before, but she loved the long white walls of colour perfume bottles in all their different shapes, sizes and prices.

She wanted to shake her head when she saw Sean walk over to the unisex (but more feminine) perfume as she knew for a fact that he was getting it for himself.

The smell of the sweet flowery perfume kept getting stronger but Bettie knew something was off. It was too strong for someone just spraying.

Bettie stared at the horribly shiny white floor and her eyes widened when she saw a smashed bottle of perfume a few metres from her.

She walked over and had to cover her nose with her hand, Bettie normally loved that perfume but it was way too strong when she was breathing in a whole bottle of it.

"You're going to have to pay for that Miss," a woman said.

Bettie looked at the tall business-like woman who had said that, and she shook her head. It was silly that this woman thought Bettie had done it, she had only just got here.

"I found it like this," Bettie said.

The woman shook her head. "They all say that. Come with me and you can pay for it at the tills,"

"I didn't break it. I'm innocent. Check your cameras,"

The woman frowned. "I know what I saw,"

Bettie couldn't believe how silly this woman was,

she supposed the woman could be fed up with all the stealing and breaking that normally happens at Christmas, but Bettie wasn't guilty.

"Aunty?" Sean said walking over.

"Sean how are you?" the woman asked. "How's Harry? We have a new stock that aftershave he likes,"

Bettie wanted to shake her head so badly, trust Sean to walk into a scene and instantly know how to calm it down. That was probably why she had bought him just in case.

"Thank you, I'll take a bottle. What were you talking to my aunty about?"

Bettie couldn't believe it when the woman looked at her and explained everything to Sean like Bettie was the worse criminal ever.

Sean nodded. "I know my Aunty seems shifty, criminal and a bit crazy but she's safe,"

How Bettie didn't playfully hit him she didn't know.

"I can assure you my Aunty didn't break anything. She's honest and she could help you,"

Bettie felt like she was going to regret this for sure, maybe she should have bought her boyfriend Graham like he had suggested.

Bettie stepped forward. "Help you how,"

"Your nephew mentions you're a Private Investigator,"

As much as Bettie wanted to correct her as she loved the more playful term Private Eye, Bettie knew this probably wasn't the time considering whoever this woman was still thought she was guilty.

"Bettie English Private Eye at your service,"

The woman nodded. "Our cameras aren't working at the moment and… my boss isn't happy with me. If I hire you to watch the store for a couple of hours-"

Bettie's mouth dropped. "Wait! I have Christmas shopping to do. I have a mini-convention to buy food for and… it's Christmas soon,"

"Aunty I can do the shopping for you,"

Bettie wanted to protest but she supposed she loved Sean too much and he was being nice, but Bettie didn't want to do this.

"How much?" Bettie asked.

"We paid the last security person a hundred pounds for the night,"

Bettie didn't know whether to be shocked, pleased or horrified that a security person is actually given that much money for a few hours of work. But the sound of a hundred pounds for two little hours, it did sound good.

It was technically her turn to host and pay for most of EyeFoodCon so that money would easily pay for it.

"Hundred pounds for the night. Extra twenty for false accusations," Bettie said.

The woman frowned.

"And throw it two bottles of whatever Sean wants since you hesitated," Bettie said smiling.

"Fine. I trust you know how to look innocent

and like a random shopper,"

As she watched the woman and Sean walk off so he could choose what he wanted, Bettie looked around the massive store and rolled her eyes. Some days it really sucked to be a private eye but a hundred pounds was a hundred pounds that she didn't have before, and maybe she could find a nice present for Graham to buy her.

The advantages of borrowing his credit card earlier!

Walking up the rows of perfume bottles, Bettie didn't know how these two hours were going to go, surely a perfume shop didn't see that much crime at Christmas.

***

After an hour and forty-five minutes, Bettie couldn't believe how brilliant this actually was, at first she thought she was going to hate it with a passion, but she didn't.

Bettie had already found some great new perfumes that she loved, she found the foul smelling one that her dad loved and she even found a new special one for herself that she might wear on Christmas day.

But Bettie still didn't want to buy any of them because as much as they were great perfumes, they weren't cheap and a hundred pounds was not going to cover it. Not by a long shot.

Bettie ran her fingers over the cold white shelves as she looked at all the perfume and aftershave bottles in all their different sizes, shapes and colours. The bottles were beautiful but Bettie remembered from her business study classes at school that was all part of the visual appeal. It did nothing practical, except from increase the prices.

The sound of customers talking, trying on perfume and judging the smells echoed all around the massive shop as Bettie waited for her two hours to be up.

Yet Bettie could have sworn there was another sound she was hearing, it was like the low quiet voices of two people conspiring to do something.

Bettie had hated the idea of people stealing from the start, it was Christmas for crying out loud, this was not a time for stealing, it was a time for love, giving and caring.

Walking to the end of the shelf she was looking at, Bettie's eyes narrowed on the two young women that were close together and trying on different perfumes.

To other people they may not have looked like criminals or would-be shoplifters, but Bettie recognised the closeness, quiet voices and the long expensive coats of the two girls.

It reminded Bettie of her own troublesome streak when she was a teenager, if that was the case with these two women then Bettie supposed she could get rid of them without any major problems.

But these women weren't teenagers, they were fully-fledged adults who were looking like they were going to try and steal something.

After a few moments of watching, Bettie noticed that one of the women had got out her phone and was pretending to take a phone call. Bettie shook her head as she watched the perfectly clear black screen of the girl's phone, if you're going to pretend to take a pretend phone call you need to make it a bit more convincing.

Bettie wondered if she should get the woman or the manager to deal with them, but she wasn't going to risk losing her hundred pounds for simply *failing* to do her assigned job. She wasn't risking any comments like that.

As the woman with the phone pretended to nod, promise the person on the other side of the call she'd take a picture and check the surroundings (completely missing Bettie). Bettie knew that this woman was an amateur, there was no way these two had done shoplifting before.

If Bettie was doing this she would have been in the car park driving home by now.

Then Bettie watched in horror as the two women did a final check of the store, missed Bettie and just picked up the perfumes like it was nothing and placed it in their coat pockets.

Bettie walked towards them. The two women pretended to act normal.

"I know what you just did," Bettie said.

"We ain't steal nothing," the pretend phone caller said.

Bettie shook her head. "I finish my 'shift' in two minutes. I do not want to be here any longer than I have to be. Just apologise, pay for the perfumes and go,"

"We ain't steal nothing," they both said together.

Bettie hated this entire thing, she had Christmas shopping to do, EyeFoodCon to plan and buy for and on top of all of that she no longer wanted to be in some perfume shop.

"Empty your pockets," Bettie said firmly.

The two women ran.

Bettie ran after them.

Her feet pounded the floor.

The two women were fast.

Bettie couldn't let them leave the shop.

She looked around.

The women were close to the exit.

There were a sea of shoppers.

Bettie was going to lose them.

Bettie panicked.

Picked up a perfume bottle.

Threw it.

It smashed on the woman's back.

She fell forward.

Catching the other woman.

There was something oddly satisfying around that Bettie realised as she walked over and stood over the two injured women were who frowning and probably wished they had tried another shop.

The tall business-like woman ran over to Bettie.

"Miss English! What have you done?"

"These two women were stealing. I stopped them. You own me my hundred pounds,"

"You damaged my store! You broke a bottle of perfume! You…"

Bettie shook her head. "My hundred pounds and extra twenty please. Or I will call your head office and tell them you hired a private eye on company time and money without approval,"

Bettie couldn't help but smile as the woman looked so shocked and panicked as if this was the first time ever she had been challenged.

"Fine Miss English," the woman said giving Bettie her money.

"Let's do this again some time," Bettie said leaving the shop.

"Let's not," Bettie heard the woman muttered.

The moment she left the shop, Bettie glided into the sea of busy grumpy shoppers and called Sean. As the phone dialled she was slightly surprised how good she was feeling after all of that, it felt great to be out in December, doing her shopping and stopping crime at the same time.

But now she had to get on with the most important event in the Private Eye calendar, EyeFoodCon.

Sean picked up his phone.

Bettie smiled. "Hi Sean, want to come to EyeFoodCon with me?"

***

A few days later Bettie sat on a terribly cold chair on the head of a long, long oak table with wonderfully decorated Christmas decorations covering the entire walls.

Bettie loved all their baubles, tinsel and the wreaths that covered the walls of the business room that she had hired especially for the convention.

And as she watched all the different Private Eyes in all their different ethnicities, sizes and heights eat the beautiful golden, crispy food in front of them, and the rest of the juicy meats and other sweet treats that covered the entire length of the table, Bettie realised something precious.

The sound of happy Private Eyes talking, chatting and laughing with one another reminded Bettie how EyeFoodCon should be explained to anyone.

Bettie looked at Sean who was laughing with a young woman at the table and he saw her.

Bettie leaned closer to Sean. "You see all this,"

Sean looked around and nodded.

"This is what EyeFoodCon is all about. No matter your race, religion, preferences, whatever. You are always welcome in the Private Eye community. We are all a family,"

Sean smiled at that.

"So what is EyeFoodCon you ask," Bettie said.

Sean leant closer.

"EyeFoodCon is about community and the secular side of Christmas. I love all Private Eyes no matter who they are and I welcome them all. This mini-convention is a reminder of that at this time of year,"

Sean looked around a final time.

"Just because we don't all celebrate Christmas doesn't mean we can't love, give and support each other at this time of year,"

Just saying that made Bettie feel all Christmassy and merry because she knew that was all the truth, and that's why she loved being a Private Eye because it truly was a community.

A loving, supporting and amazing community for all.

Bettie was a bit surprised when Sean kissed her cheek and held her hands.

"Merry Christmas Aunty,"

Bettie stood up and said to everyone: "A Merry Christmas, New Year and all the other celebrations to everyone,"

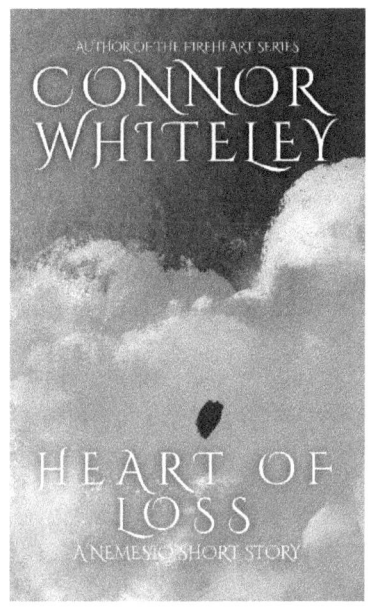

GET YOUR FREE AND EXCLUSIVE SHORT STORY NOW! LEARN ABOUT NEMESIO'S PAST!

https://www.subscribepage.com/fireheart

About the author:

Connor Whiteley is the author of over 60 books in the sci-fi fantasy, nonfiction psychology and books for writer's genre and he is a Human Branding Speaker and Consultant.

He is a passionate warhammer 40,000 reader, psychology student and author.

Who narrates his own audiobooks and he hosts The Psychology World Podcast.

All whilst studying Psychology at the University of Kent, England.

Also, he was a former Explorer Scout where he gave a speech to the Maltese President in August 2018 and he attended Prince Charles' 70th Birthday Party at Buckingham Palace in May 2018.

Plus, he is a self-confessed coffee lover!

More From The Holiday Extravaganza:

Criminal Christmas:
Crime, Christmas, Closet
Protecting Christmas
Christmas Thief
Christmas, Crime, letter
Private Eye, Convention and Christmas
Cheater At Dinner
Perfect Christmas
Salvation In The Maid
Criminal, Resistance, Alliance
Dark Farm
Great Give Away

Sweet Christmas
Lights, Love, Christmas
Journalist, Zookeeper, Love
Young Romantic Hearts
Love In The Newspaper
Holiday, Burnout, Love
Homeless, Charity, Love
Cold December Night
Driving Home For Love
Love At The Winter Wedding
Fireworks, New Year, Love
Loving In The New Year Tourist

Fantastical Christmas:
Magic That Binds
One Final Christmas
Author's Christmas Problems
Last Winter Dragon Egg
A Sacrifice For Saturnalia
Soulcaster
Weird First Christmas
All Feast
Solstice Guardian
Wheel of Years
Repent

OTHER SHORT STORIES BY CONNOR WHITELEY

Mystery Short Stories:
Poison In The Candy Cane
Christmas Innocence
You Better Watch Out
Christmas Theft
Trouble In Christmas
Smell of The Lake
Problem In A Car
Theft, Past and Team
Embezzler In The Room
A Strange Way To Go
A Horrible Way To Go
Ann Awful Way To Go
An Old Way To Go
A Fishy Way To Go
A Pointy Way To Go
A High Way To Go
A Fiery Way To Go
A Glassy Way To Go
A Chocolatey Way To Go
Kendra Detective Mystery Collection Volume 1
Kendra Detective Mystery Collection Volume 2
Stealing A Chance At Freedom

Glassblowing and Death
Theft of Independence
Cookie Thief
Marble Thief
Book Thief
Art Thief
Mated At The Morgue
The Big Five Whoopee Moments
Stealing An Election
Mystery Short Story Collection Volume 1
Mystery Short Story Collection Volume 2

Science Fiction Short Stories:
The First Rememberer
Life of A Rememberer
System of Wonder
Lifesaver
Remarkable Way She Died
The Interrogation of Annabella Stormic
Blade of The Emperor
Arbiter's Truth
Computation of Battle
Old One's Wrath
Puppets and Masters
Ship of Plague
Interrogation
Edge of Failure

One Way Choice
Acceptable Losses
Balance of Power
Good Idea At The Time
Escape Plan
Escape In The Hesitation
Inspiration In Need
Singing Warriors
Knowledge is Power
Killer of Polluters
Climate of Death
The Family Mailing Affair
Defining Criminality
The Martian Affair
A Cheating Affair
The Little Café Affair
Mountain of Death
Prisoner's Fight
Claws of Death
Bitter Air
Honey Hunt
Blade On A Train

Fantasy Short Stories:
City of Snow
City of Light
City of Vengeance

Dragons, Goats and Kingdom
Smog The Pathetic Dragon
Don't Go In The Shed
The Tomato Saver
The Remarkable Way She Died
The Bloodied Rose
Asmodia's Wrath
Heart of A Killer
Emissary of Blood
Dragon Coins
Dragon Tea
Dragon Rider
Sacrifice of the Soul
Heart of The Flesheater
Heart of The Regent
Heart of The Standing
Feline of The Lost
Heart of The Story
City of Fire
Awaiting Death

Other books by Connor Whiteley:
Bettie English Private Eye Series
A Very Private Woman
The Russian Case
A Very Urgent Matter
A Case Most Personal
Trains, Scots and Private Eyes
The Federation Protects

The Fireheart Fantasy Series
Heart of Fire
Heart of Lies
Heart of Prophecy
Heart of Bones
Heart of Fate

City of Assassins (Urban Fantasy)
City of Death
City of Marytrs
City of Pleasure
City of Power

Agents of The Emperor
Return of The Ancient Ones
Vigilance
Angels of Fire
Kingmaker

The Garro Series- Fantasy/Sci-fi
GARRO: GALAXY'S END
GARRO: RISE OF THE ORDER
GARRO: END TIMES
GARRO: SHORT STORIES
GARRO: COLLECTION
GARRO: HERESY
GARRO: FAITHLESS
GARRO: DESTROYER OF WORLDS
GARRO: COLLECTIONS BOOK 4-6
GARRO: MISTRESS OF BLOOD
GARRO: BEACON OF HOPE
GARRO: END OF DAYS

Winter Series- Fantasy Trilogy Books
WINTER'S COMING
WINTER'S HUNT
WINTER'S REVENGE
WINTER'S DISSENSION

Miscellaneous:
RETURN
FREEDOM
SALVATION
Reflection of Mount Flame
The Masked One
The Great Deer

www.ingramcontent.com/pod-product-compliance
Lightning Source LLC
LaVergne TN
LVHW011856060526
838200LV00054B/4355